Sylis Michael Alexander

For my
first-born
grandson...

...and his
gorgeous
parents who
made him.

Happy 3ʳᵈ
birthday
beautiful
boy!

Sylis Michael Alexander is a strong boy.

He likes to watch movies and play with his toys.

He will grow
up to be a
big, tall,
strong man.

And maybe
squeeze
walnuts
open with
one hand!

He'll be big like his daddy and uncles one day.

He will be
big enough
to scare
monsters
away!!

Mommyy!! The human is scaring me!!

He likes to
run, jump,
and swing.

He likes

to

skateboard...

..and

does

tricks

on the

thing!

He was
flipping a
skateboard

when he was
really little.

He likes

to eat

snacks...

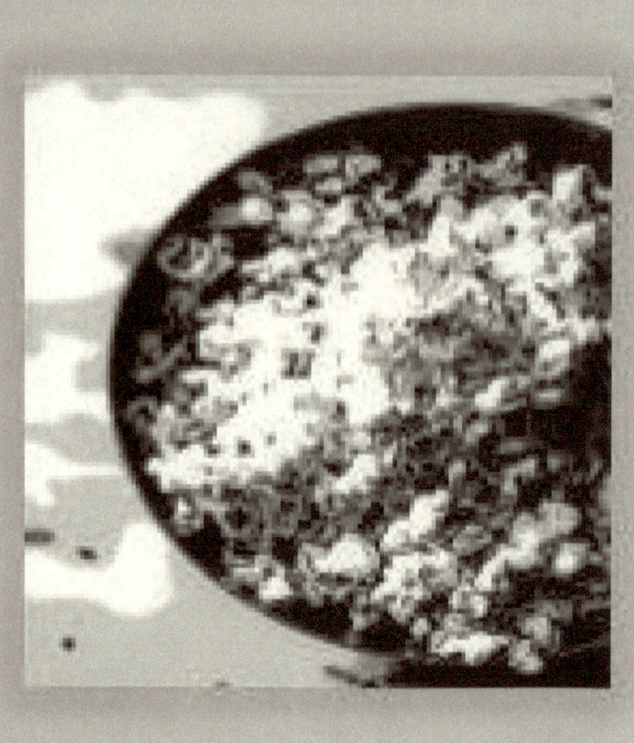

...and for
supper,
he eats
vittles!

He has more
gramma's
and
grandpa's

than any
kid I've
ever
known.

When
you hear
how
many he
has,

your

mind will

surely

be

blown!

He has
Great Great
Grandma,
Great Great
Gramma O,
Nanny and
Great Grandma
Judy.

All are so
very uniquely
special and
also are
absolute
beauties.

He has
Great Pawpaw
and
Great Grandpa Ron,
Great Abuela Amalia,
and
Great Papa Don.

There is
Granny,
PawPaw,
Gramma,
Papa, Nana.

Papaw
and
Mamaw
and
Pop-Pop
and
Gämma.

Then last
but not least
there is
Poppy and
Gramgram.

Boy, that is
a really
gigantic big
fam,
fam!

He has just
one brother.

He's the
best brother
by far!

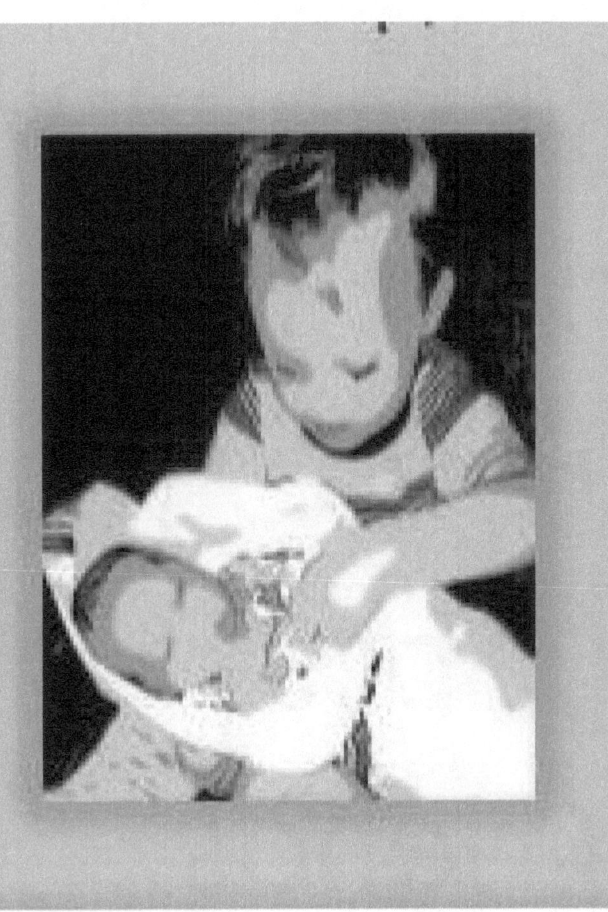

He's a baby
right now,
but they'll be
best
friends...

wishing

on

stars.

There

are

aunties

and

uncles

and

cousins

galore.

First cousins, second cousins,

third

and

then

four!

He has a

really

big

family...

that is
for sure!

But
there is
so much
love

that is

so very

pure.

When you
have this
much love...

...you feel

quite like a

King.

With a big family behind you, you can do ANYthing!

Doctor
MailMan
President
Lawyer
Firefighter
CEO
Captian
Pilot
Painter
Teacher
Investigator
Chemist
Judge
Entertainer
Construction
worker
Chef
Secret
Agent

He has
got lots
of cool
talent

and a

family

that's

BIG

Sylis
Michael
Alexander

sure is

one

special

kid!

The End

~~~~~~~
~~~~~~~

Good Night

sleep tight

❤ Gämma ❤

loves you

Grand Bunny

Draw your own
pictures on the
following pages.

~~~~~~

~~~~~~

trebel bass publishing ™